Away Goes Sally

SALLY
1790

AWAY GOES SALLY

BY

ELIZABETH COATSWORTH

PICTURES BY

HELEN SEWELL

Bethlehem Books • Ignatius Press
Bathgate, N.D. San Francisco

Cover art © by Roseanne Sharpe
Cover design by Davin Carlson

ISBN 1-883937-83-3
Library of Congress Card Number: 2003110233

Bethlehem Books • Ignatius Press
10194 Garfield Street South
Bathgate, North Dakota 58216
800-757-6831
www.bethlehembooks.com

Printed in the United States on acid-free paper.

FOR MARRAINE

Also by Elizabeth Coatsworth

Stories about Sally

Away Goes Sally
Five Bushel Farm
The Fair American
The White Horse
The Wonderful Day

Historical Stories

The Golden Horseshoe
Sword of the Wilderness
You Shall Have a Carriage
Dancing Tom
Door to the North
The Last Fort
Jon the Unlucky
The Hand of Apollo
George and Red
American Adventures 1620-1945
First Adventure
The Wishing Pear
Boston Bells
Aunt Flora
Old Whirlwind: A Story of Davy Crockett
The Sod House
Cherry Ann and the Dragon Horse

Others

The Cat Who Went to Heaven (Newbery Medal)
Alice All by Herself
The Littlest House
Houseboat Summer
Thief Island
Jock's Island

Poetry for Children

Night and the Cat
Mouse Chores
The Peaceable Kingdom and other Poems
The Children Come Running
The Sparrow Bush: Rhymes
Down Half the World

And many others

Contents

Illustrations

1. *The Salt Hay*

AUNT DEBORAH, the "middle" aunt, thought it was dangerous. Gay young Aunt Esther thought Sally was quite old enough.

"The child's very sensible, Sister Deborah, and strong in the wrists," she said. "What do you think, Sister Nannie?"

It was Aunt Nannie who decided almost everything in the household. She was the eldest of the three aunts, short and solid, with red cheeks and black eyes under straight brows, and such energy that she could scarcely speak without making her gold ear-drops jingle.

"Of course the child is old enough to drive alone to the salt meadows," she answered briskly. "Esther, you help her harness Dorcas, while Deborah and I finish packing the meadow victuals. Salt haying, I always say, is the hungriest work of the whole year."

Soon Sally was in the two-wheeled gig with the great hamper of provisions under the seat, driving slowly down the road.

"Mind you don't let Dorcas more than just trot, child!" Aunt Deborah called after her. But Sally was in no hurry. She was filled with a sense of adventure—partly the adventure of her first drive alone, but more than that, a sense of something that was going to happen. She couldn't help feeling glad that it was baking day, with a big wash bleaching on the hedge, and the cheeses to be rubbed, and the vegetables to be picked, and the extra haying work, to keep the aunts at home just for this one day.

Dorcas trotted on, *clup-clup-clupper-clup*, each step raising a puff of dust. At Jordan Farm, Sally caught a glimpse of Mrs. Jordan in the cheese room and waved. The hedges of chokecherry and elderberry between the road and the stone walls were whitened with the dust of late summer. The goldenrod plumes nodded above gray leaves, and the sun was hot and dry. Under the willows by the brook she pulled Dorcas to a walk. She loved the big trees with their small dark leaves in which a few wisps of hay had caught from the passing wagons. It was cool there.

Once out of the shadow of the willows, Dorcas trotted again up the hill into the village, past the Bell-and-Sixpence Tavern, and then by a winding road to the edge of the salt meadows where the hay grew wild in the marshes. The noon-day sun hung overhead, and the hay was almost burningly bright between the channels of blue salt water. Though the sea itself was out of sight, the smell of it hung strong and fresh in the air, and the trim gulls were drifting overhead. Their shadows went sliding across the hay, sometimes darkening for a moment the hands of the men working there.

Sally knew just where to look for Uncle Joseph and Uncle Eben and the three hired men, and quickly recognized their group from among the others at work. Uncle Joseph was leading the mowing with long steady sweeps of his arms, each ending in a sort of jerk, walking forward through a continual slow falling wave of grass and a hiss of steel on dry stalks. The other men had hard work to keep up with him. Uncle Eben had dropped behind and was honing the curved blade of his scythe.

"To cut well, you must sharpen well," he used to say with a sly wink at Sally. He was fat and lazy. He spent more time sharpening than cutting, but people liked to work with him because he was always jolly.

It was Uncle Eben who first saw the gig and waved his hat.

"Dinner, lads!" he called and scrambled nimbly up the steep bank to the road. In a moment he had Dorcas tied, and Sally swung out, and the big hamper in its place on the grass. By the time Uncle Joseph and the hired men had hung their scythes in a maple crotch and joined them under the trees, Sally had spread a clean cloth and put out the baked beans, corned beef, mince pie, doughnuts, and plumcake which the aunts had packed with last year's perry, a sort of cider made from their own pears, and a jug of Jamaica.

"There's no one can vie with Miss Nannie's fixin's," said one of the men, a neighbor who was through with his own haying and was ready to hire out now to help Uncle Joseph.

"Have some more beef," said Uncle Eben. "You're all 'way behind me. Joseph may lead at the mowing, but I lead at the eating."

"You had a head start, Eben," said Uncle Joseph.

"Head and heels," chuckled Uncle Eben. "Little Sally will never have to wait for me. I hope she will be able to say the same of all her beaux."

Sally sat laughing with the others, cutting cake and big slices of pie for them, and nibbling away like a little black-eyed mouse. She was happy, but she was still waiting for something—something far-off now, like a bird whose color and shape she could not yet make out. But it would come nearer in good time. Meanwhile she loved sitting with the men under the trees. Here and there other haying parties were eating in groups. There was much laughter and calling back and forth, one set taunting another for being behind in the work. Each large farm had a share of the meadow, marked off by stakes, not at all like the usual fields, for these grew of their own accord and were harvested in a sort of hard-working picnic, within smell of the sea. Bringing in the salt hay marked the end of summer. The English hay was already in, and the grain was reaped and the flax pulled. It was the jolly time of the year, a contented time when Uncle Joseph no longer watched for rain, and Aunt Nannie went about smiling. She knew that the cellar was full of potatoes and turnips, and the hanging shelves stocked with berry preserves and pickles, and the great chest in the spinning chamber stored with wheat, rye, oats, and barley for the winter months.

As Sally drove home she saw old Captain Dagget in one of the fields, his hair powdered in a queue, his gun lying beside him under the fence. He waved at her and she waved back. He had fought in the Revolution, and the years of hardship and bloodshed had turned him a little queer so that he still thought the Redcoats might be coming down the road.

"Seen anything of them Britishers, Miss Sally?" he called to her.

"Didn't pass any, Captain Dagget," she called back, and drove on.

The three aunts were sitting in the back room by the open door overlooking the new-mown field dotted by apple trees. They had on their calico dresses and their brooches, in case company came, and Sally saw that they had out their company sewing. As soon as she had unharnessed Dorcas, she ran up to her room and put on a fresh blue and white gingham. The cloth was homemade, but Aunt Deborah had taught her how to starch and she thought it looked very well. For a moment after bringing her chair beside her aunts she sat doing nothing but enjoying the smells—a smell of hay, a smell of late roses by the door, a smell of starch, a smell of birchwood smoke, a faint smell of lavender from Aunt Deborah's dress. The cloud shadows moved peacefully across the field. She could hear a horse's hoof-beats ringing hollow on the bridge down the road.

"I'm so happy!" she exclaimed.

"Seen anything of them Britishers, Miss Sally?"

"I should think so, child!" said Aunt Nannie, her eardrops jingling, her needle flying in and out of the cambric she was hemming.

Sally picked up her work, a half-finished straw bonnet. She had braided the straw very smoothly and evenly and now was stitching it into shape. It would be too late to wear this year, but she would have it in the spring with a white ribbon. As she worked she listened idly to the horse. Instead of passing by as she expected, the animal turned at their lane, and she heard their Dorcas whinny.

"Go see who it is, child," said Aunt Nannie, never pausing in her work.

It might be anyone on any errand, yet as Sally jumped to her feet she had a feeling that the thing was now about to happen, falling like a stone into the quiet pool of the afternoon. In a moment she ran back, her cheeks pink with the hurry, and a folded and sealed letter in her hands.

"It was the post," she cried excitedly, for the post seldom stopped at their door. "I asked him to alight and take something to eat and drink, but he was in a hurry and could not stop."

Aunt Nannie took the letter.

"For Brother Joseph," she remarked, "from Cousin

Ephraim Hallet who went to Maine. Well, well, child, letters have been written before this, and will be again. Put it there on the table until your uncle comes and let us go on with our sewing. It will soon be time to milk."

But though Sally picked up her bonnet once more and listened to the conversation of her aunts, her thoughts remained on the letter that lay behind her, full of mystery. And it seemed to her that the aunts were waiting, too, waiting for Uncle Joseph to come home and the letter to be opened.

This is the hay that no man planted,
This is the ground that was never plowed,
Watered by tides, cold and brackish,
Shadowed by fog and the sea-born cloud.

Here comes no sound of bobolink's singing,
Only the wail of the gull's long cry,
Where men now reap as they reap their meadows
Heaping the great gold stacks to dry.

All winter long when deep pile the snowdrifts,
And cattle stand in the dark all day,
Many a cow shall taste pale sea-weed
Twined in the stalks of the wild salt hay.

2. *The Letter*

THE EVENING had grown cool and the aunts put out the rye bread and cheese and the bowls of new milk for supper on the long kitchen table. The fire in the big fireplace was welcome, taking off the chill of the evening air. A new moon hung in a sky that was turning green above the barn weathervane. The cows were all in their stalls and the milk was drawn in the wooden pails before the men came home from the salt meadows.

"You have a letter, Brother Joseph," said Aunt Esther eagerly when the uncles came in. She was only twenty, pretty and full of curiosity.

"Don't talk to a hungry man about letters, my dear," put in Aunt Nannie, jingling her ear-drops. She was curious, too, but as the eldest sister she felt it was her duty to reprove Aunt Esther. "Sit down, Brother Joseph. Sally, bring your Uncle Eben a spoon. There, you had a good day for the hay, I expect."

"The haying was all very well, Sister," said Uncle Eben with one of his mischievous looks, "but where was the apple pie for tea? You broke your promise, Nannie! And you can't expect a man to do his best mowing without his favorite pie."

"You ate it for breakfast, Brother, and well you know it," said Aunt Nannie, smiling at him, "but I declare it makes baking easy to have a person love his victuals as you do."

"Who is the letter from?" asked Uncle Joseph. He was sitting in the ladder-back armchair between the green of the evening light at the window and the rose of the fire-light on the hearth. Sally, eating her bread and milk as she perched on the children's bench by the red oven door in the fireplace, looked at him admiringly. He was like a mast in a ship, round and strong, and though he could be obstinate and masterful at times, he was always gentle with her.

"It is from Cousin Ephraim Hallet, Brother Joseph," said Aunt Esther quickly.

"At least, so we suppose, Brother," added Aunt Deborah, who was seldom quite certain of things.

Sally jumped up too and brought a candle.

"Oho! So that's why you are so interested, Esther?" exclaimed Uncle Eben, looking at Aunt Esther knowingly. Then Sally remembered that Cousin Ephraim's brother Samuel used to take Aunt Esther riding before they moved to Maine.

"Bring me the wonderful letter, my dear," Uncle Joseph said to Aunt Esther, and Sally jumped up too and brought a candle.

Uncle Joseph broke the seal with a brown forefinger, and read:

My dearest Cousin,

I hope that this finds you and all our cousins and little Sally as well as it leaves us. We have prospered amazingly in this new country on the Penobscot River. Sam and I have already cleared thirty acres of good valley land, and by next year we hope to have a frame house standing. At present we are content with one of logs, with a roof of bark, and a fireplace of field-stone, with clay and wattles for the chimney. Our rooms are curtained off with quilts, and Jennie says that she can see daylight through the chinks in the oven, but I notice that her doughnuts and pies are as good as they were in Hingham. There is no proper school for John and Sophronia, but a young lady from Salem, a sister of one of our neighbors, teaches the children every morning in her brother's home. There is no tuition, but Jennie says that she is intending to give her her muff and tippet for her pains, and truly Sophronia's writing has greatly improved.

I have an Indian boy working for me. He does well with the cattle though no great hand with an axe. Still, he is diligent and faithful. There are many Indians hereabouts and often they come to sleep by our kitchen fire, and they have never stolen so much as a hen, having on the other hand more often brought us a present of deer's meat in return for what Jennie gives them from her cooking. Our white neighbors are very superior. Next to us is a judge, and there are lawyers and divines as well as farmers and artisans from the older settlements. The saw-mill is already built and a meeting house, and next year I hear there is to be an ordinary. Every man who will erect buildings is given fifty acres outright, and land is cheap. The timber is fine, the soil excellent. I raise twice as much wheat to the acre as I could on the old farm. The climate is healthy though the winters are long, and John has recovered from the cough that troubled him. Here there is much more opportunity than at home. Jennie says that she prefers being the head of the poor to being the tail of the rich, and she expects me to become a great man in this new country, let alone what John is to be.

I write so much in detail, my dear Cousin, because it has occurred to me that you and your brother Eben and your sisters might come here, too, taking up some very good land that may still be had near us. Here you could own as far as you can see, looking down upon a prospect of river and hills, and living like a squire. We could wish that you might come soon.

In hopes that some day we may be neighbors as well as cousins,
I remain,
Your very obedt servt,

EPHRAIM HALLET

Postcript.

Jennie says to tell cousin Deborah that all her roses she brought with her have thriven, and Sophronia adds I must tell her dearest Sally she shall have a bear-cub like her own Antic.

E.H.

"An uncivilized wilderness if ever there was one!" exclaimed Aunt Nannie sharply and her knitting needles clicked over the stockings she was making. "I suppose our cousins wear moccasins and feathers, to hear Ephraim talk. What nonsense to think we would leave our farm for a lot of woods filled with yowling savages!"

"I don't know, Nannie," said Uncle Joseph mildly. "I have long been considering something of the kind."

Sally jumped up and down on her bench with excitement, and Aunt Esther took a sudden breath. But Aunt Nannie said, firmly, "Nonsense, Brother!"

"Why nonsense?" asked Uncle Eben who loved to tease.

"This is where we were born, and this is where I expect us to die," said Aunt Nannie solemnly.

"We hope to live a long time first, Nannie," said Uncle Joseph, "and in a new country we could prosper more. There are too many people here and the land is wearing out. I get nothing like the crops we got in our father's time. If it's the house you cling to, you shall have a finer one on the Penobscot, all in good time. Eben, are you willing to go?"

"Yes, so long as you don't expect me to walk there, Brother," said Uncle Eben, twinkling and twiddling his thumbs.

"Esther?"

"Yes, Brother Joseph," said Aunt Esther, very low.

"Deborah?"

"I don't know what to say, Brother Joseph, between you and Sister Nannie, indeed I don't," and gentle Aunt Deborah began to cry.

Aunt Nannie did not wait to be asked. "They may all say and do what they will, but I tell you plain, Joseph, I shall not go flitting about in wretched taverns eating dirty food and sleeping in dirtier beds. The rest of you may go, but the child and I stay here where we belong."

Sally's face fell. She had already seen herself wrapped in furs driving behind Dorcas through the woods, the sleighbells jingling, seeing new things and meeting new people every day. If only Aunt Nannie would not be so set against it! She jumped up from her bench and ran over to her aunt and put her arms about her neck.

"Oh, please, please, Aunt Nannie, let us go to the Penobscot, and I can have a little bear and play with Sophronia and the Indian children."

"That would not be a very genteel upbringing, I am afraid, child," said Aunt Nannie, her ear-drops jingling. "No, my dear, you stay here."

"Sister," said Uncle Joseph, "I tell you plain I am going, and you cannot get on here without me."

He stood up very tall and big, facing Aunt Nannie with a frown.

Aunt Nannie too stood up, shaking her skirts into place angrily while her curls bobbed.

"Brother," she said, facing him like a small cat facing a mastiff, "I tell you plain I shall never leave my own house, nor shall Sally, whose mother left her especially in my charge. And now, good-night to you all and pleasant dreams," and she bustled out of the room.

The axe has cut the forest down,
The laboring ox has smoothed all clear,
Apples now grow where pine trees stood,
And slow cows graze instead of deer.

Where Indian fires once raised their smoke
The chimneys of a farmhouse stand,
And cocks crow barnyard challenges
To dawns that once saw savage land.

The axe, the plow, the binding wall,
By these the wilderness is tamed,
By these the white man's will is wrought,
The rivers bridged, the new towns named.

3. *The Six Little Pots*

SALLY SAT on the doorstep of unhewn stone watching the pink four-o'clocks. They were almost all out now. It was time to get tea. Of course she could have looked at the grandfather's clock by the stairs, but it was more fun telling time by the flowers which Aunt Deborah always kept growing in the dooryard.

"Miss Deborah has the green thumb," old Mrs. Captain Dagget always said. "She can make anything grow, I declare. It's a gift."

To-day Sally was getting the tea alone, for Miss Eliza Dagget and Mrs. Caleb Parker, her sister, were sitting in the front room with the aunts.

She raked the hot embers into six mounds and put on six small iron pots: coffee for Uncle Joseph, chocolate for Uncle Eben, who loved sweets, strong old Hyson tea for Aunt Nannie, weak Hyson for Aunt Deborah, and

Souchong for Aunt Esther. Sally had a little pot of her own which Uncle Eben brought her one day from Boston.

"You're turning into a little black-eyed witch, child," he said, "and you shall have your own pot and make your own brew."

And so she too had her own chocolate like Uncle Eben's, but with more milk in it.

While the water was boiling, she spread the table, made cream toast, and laid out a loaf of new bread, a big pat of butter, gooseberry preserves, apple and cherry pie, and doughnuts. She was using the luster china from England and the silver fiddle-back spoons, so thin that she had always to be careful not to bend them.

She would call the uncles first, for they would have to wash. She stood at the back door and watched them a moment carrying baskets of corn-ears into the barn, bending back to balance the weight. The yoke of oxen and the cart stood in the September sunlight. On a sudden impulse she ran out and gave the beasts each an ear of corn to munch. They watched her kindly from their dark eyes, and she saw the late sunlight shining ember-red through their ears.

"Will you please come in for tea, Uncle Joseph? I

She raked the hot embers into six mounds
and put on six small iron pots.

needn't ask you, Uncle Eben!" she added mischievously.

"I've been awaiting that word ever since dinner, my dear," said Uncle Eben.

Uncle Joseph was quieter than usual. Neither he nor Aunt Nannie had said much to each other for the last ten days, but sometimes they looked as though they were measuring each other's wills. Uncle Joseph still assumed that they were emigrating. Aunt Nannie took pains to lay plans for the farm for the next year and the year after that.

When Sally opened the parlor door the ladies were talking of Maine. With a bustle of putting away their go-abroad knitting, they trooped out to the table.

"Our Cousin Ephraim is quite in raptures over the country," said Aunt Esther, looking at Aunt Nannie a little defiantly. Sally looked too. She wished Aunt Nannie wouldn't shut her mouth in a straight line and pinch in her nostrils. They all wanted to go—even Aunt Deborah. Sally had found her looking at an old atlas and tracing the rivers with her finger. But Aunt Nannie would never give in.

"I have told my brother," she was saying now in her solemnest way, emphasizing the words with such nods of her head that her ear-drops danced, "and I will tell you all, I will never leave my own fire nor sleep in any but my own bed."

"And I say," said Uncle Joseph firmly, "that go to the Penobscot we shall, and Nannie with us."

Uncle Joseph and Aunt Nannie looked at each other and their eyes flashed.

"Now what will you have, ladies?" cried Uncle Eben cheerfully. "My chocolate is the best, but there is a wide choice."

"I wish I knew how it will end!" said Aunt Esther in a low voice to Mrs. Caleb, who was her particular friend.

Mrs. Caleb's eyes sparkled. "Go ask Tuggie Noyes," she said, laughing. "Tuggie Noyes will know."

"Do let us go, Aunt Esther," whispered Sally, who had overheard. "May I go with you? I've never visited a witch. Will she give us tea?"

"Shh, child," said Aunt Esther, but Sally noticed that she did not say "no." The talk closed over the idea like water over a tossed pebble, but Sally could see it still shining clear and bright through all the laughter and gossip. Uncle Eben was very attentive to Miss Eliza. People always said he would have courted her if it hadn't been too much trouble. During tea a wind had sprung up, swinging the weathervane around. By the time the visitors had found their cloaks and put their knitting in their embroidered hanging pockets, it was blowing hard and the trees were turning the pale sides of their leaves to the sky and rustling dryly as though they were afraid.

"We had best drive you home," said Uncle Joseph, standing beside them at the door.

But Miss Eliza and her sister laughed.

"You must get in your corn before it rains," they said. "The wind will be our chaise and carry us home in four minutes. Good-bye, good-bye, good-bye!" And they were off, with the wind blowing their red cloaks and hurrying them down the path by the stone wall.

Sally stood waving for a moment, and then, catching Aunt Esther's hand, ran into the wind towards the upper pasture, where the cows were already gathered by the bars, waiting for milking time and the dark shelter of the barn.

Hard from the southeast blows the wind
Promising rain.
The clouds are gathering, and dry leaves
Tap at the pane.

Early the cows come wandering home
To shadowy bars,
Early the candles are alight
And a few stars.

Now is the hour that lies between
Bright day and night,
When in the dusk the fire blooms
In tongues of light,

And the cat comes to bask herself
In the soft heat,
And Madame Peace draws up her chair
To warm her feet.

4. *The Witch*

DAYS WENT by and still Sally heard no word about visiting the witch. The pumpkins were in, the ox was stalled and fattening for Thanksgiving, and soon the old tailor would come with his goose and stay several days making the uncles' coats and trousers for the winter. One fine evening the Daggets and some other neighbors came after milking for a corn-husking. The men sat on the floor of the barn in the light of the hunter's moon, stripping the husks from the yellow ears of corn, talking and joking and sometimes singing. It was cold outdoors but Sally made excuses to run to the barn on errands to see the work going on so merrily in the big square of moonlight, while the cows breathed quietly somewhere in the darkness beyond and the hay from the lofts smelled like dried summer.

But soon Aunt Nannie appeared in the door of the house and called her.

"Stay with the females, child," she said when Sally came. And Sally, giving a last look at the silver world outside, followed her aunt obediently into the kitchen. The ladies were seated about the fireplace on rush-bottomed chairs, peeling and slicing fruit in the warmth and sparkle of the fire. The whole big room smelled of apples and pears and quinces, standing in big baskets, or sliced and juicy in the kettles and bowls that ringed the hearth. If fingers flew, tongues flew faster, and Sally noticed that Aunt Esther and Mrs. Caleb were whispering and nodding together.

The days went busily by. When she came home from school she joined her aunts in the back chamber upstairs where they were weaving whenever they had a spare minute so that the woolen cloth might be finished and dyed at the mill and be back in time to be made up for Thanksgiving.

She was old enough to reel the yarn that would be knitted into stockings during the long winter evenings. Forty yards to a reel—she measured it with a sort of song, beating out the time:

"There's one,
There ain't one,
There will be one
By 'n' by—"

while the big flies buzzed in the window. Ten verses, and she snapped the yarn. The reel was wound.

One afternoon when the day's weaving was finished Aunt Esther caught Sally's eye.

"Will you come for a walk with me, child?" she asked. "We'll go down the road a piece and see if we can encounter any of Captain Dagget's Redcoats."

Sally jumped to her feet and ran for their bonnets. Hand in hand they walked down the lane.

"Where are you going, Esther?" Aunt Nannie called after them, but Aunt Esther only laughed and waved her hand.

Up the road they walked, crossed the brook at the stepping-stones, and turned off at the hill road. The trees grew close on either side and the ruts were deep and muddy. The woods were full of crows flying from tree to tree, black and cawing. For a mile they passed nothing but tumbled stone walls and a clearing where a blackened chimney stood above a cellar hole, and the young pines were growing up among forgotten apple trees.

"Is Tuggie Noyes really a witch, Aunt Esther?" asked Sally, holding tight to her aunt's hand.

"I don't know, Sally," said Aunt Esther, and her voice, usually so gay, was a little uncertain. "Perhaps it is getting late. We will call another day."

"Oh, pray, Aunt Esther, now that we are almost there, let us go on!" cried Sally who the moment before had been dreading the visit, but now was in terror only for fear it might not take place. "We *must* find out if we shall emigrate, and whether Uncle Joseph or Aunt Nannie shall have the victory."

Aunt Esther nodded without speaking. And now they came to a small clearing with a little house in it and flowers still bright at the door.

"See Tuggie Noyes' flowers, Aunt Esther!" whispered Sally. "The frost has not touched them."

"The woods protect them, child," said Aunt Esther, but Sally noticed that she drew back her skirts so that they should not touch the flowers by the doorstep as she knocked.

There was a stir within. Then complete silence. Round the corner of the house came a black chicken. Beak and claws had been clipped. It stood in the path and stared at them, then disappeared whence it had come, and they heard a door open and the chicken clucking.

"It's telling her who we are," whispered Sally. She had always heard of the hen who was Tuggie Noyes' familiar, but this was the first time she had ever seen it.

The door swung open. Tuggie Noyes stood curtseying to them.

"What may I do for you, Miss Esther?" she asked. "Or is it Miss Sally who is ailing? The child looks pale." And she smiled at Sally, a slightly malicious smile that showed her teeth. Tuggie Noyes' teeth were not like other people's. They were all double teeth and it gave her a curious appearance. She was a heavy dark woman in middle age, dressed in an old damask gown that had been very fine but was now torn and dirtied. Sally had seen her at the Daggets', helping with the weaving, but it was different now, at the door of her own house.

Aunt Esther cleared her throat.

"We have come, Mrs. Noyes, to ask you a question," she managed to say.

Her voice did not quite sound like her own.

Tuggie Noyes curtseyed again.

"Come in, Miss Esther. Come in, Miss Sally," she said.

"I know your question, but ask it, ask it."

Her parlor was dark and crowded. There was a queer odor in it which Sally did not know. The chairs had been fine, like Tuggie Noyes' dress, and were too large for the room, and covered with backs and seats of wool-work, and the andirons had iron negroes' heads on them with glass eyes that winked in the firelight. The black hen was standing on the hearth watching them as they came in.

Tuggie Noyes motioned to two chairs and sat down herself.

"So you come asking after Maine?" she said. "Shall you go north? And who wins, tug Joseph, tug Nannie? Well, I'll answer you more than you ask. There'll be a wedding before the leaves turn yellow again in my woods, and they each shall win."

Aunt Esther looked self-conscious, and it was Sally who said:

"But, ma'am, how may both win?"

"I answer questions, but do not explain my answers, child," replied the witch sharply. "And now may I trouble you, Miss Esther, for two shillings? I hear old Crumple-Horn calling me."

As Aunt Esther fumbled in her hanging pocket for the money, they could indeed hear a cow mooing, but

"I'll answer questions but do not explain my answers, child."

Sally was sure there had been no sound at all when Tuggie Noyes first spoke of it.

"She *is* a witch," thought Sally, and, astonished at her own daring, she dropped sixpence behind her as she walked out of the door after her aunt. But Tuggie Noyes followed them over the sixpence, then turned and picked it up, calling Sally back.

"You dropped this, child," she said, grinning, and the black hen on the hearth broke into a loud cackling.

"Thank you, ma'am," Sally answered steadily, taking the money. The sixpence had not stopped Tuggie. Then either she was not a witch after all or the charm didn't work. No witch could walk over a sixpence, people said. The black chicken came stepping on its toes out of the door.

"Curtsey for the little miss, Jessica," said Tuggie Noyes, and the hen bobbed and ducked, spreading its wings.

"Come, Sally," called Aunt Esther from the gate, and Sally pulled her gaze from the clipped-bill hen, and ran down the path towards Aunt Esther, feeling the eyes of the old woman and of the chicken fixed on her back. She caught Aunt Esther's hand, and without looking round again they hurried off down the road.

A chickadee called from a pine tree, and a maple leaf, clear-cut and scarlet, fluttered down towards them through the still air. Aunt Esther went more slowly, and Sally saw that she was smiling a little to herself, but she only said gaily, "How can they both win, Sally? *There's* a riddle that's not in the almanac."

When the pumpkin yellows
And the standing corn
Is pale with frost, and cobwebs
Hang silver in the morn,

When Orion rises
Over fields cut bare,
And the fallen apples
Smell cidery on the air,

Then comes the witches' Sabbath
Of the flocking crows;
Standing by the barn door,
Every farmer knows

When he hears that clangor,
Sees that windy flight,
Winter soon is coming,
Cold, and early night.

5. *Uncle Joseph Has An Idea*

IT WAS Indian summer. The crows walked in the stubble, and a blue haze hung in the leafless woods day after day. Uncle Joseph and Uncle Eben went about preparing for the long winter, making sure that the barns were tight and the hemlock branches heaped about the house to help keep the floors warm. The pigs were killed, and puddings and sausages made, and the hams hung to cure in the wide kitchen fireplace. Sometimes when she was not in school Sally went with Uncle Joseph into the woods while he got sand to repair the lanes. Sometimes they had their meal together there, a simple meal of spring water drunk from the hollow of their hands, and bread and cheese which Uncle Joseph pared with his knife.

One sunny day she had wandered off, walking quietly through the windless trees, when she heard Uncle Joseph whistling for her. She ran back to where he stood by the ox-sled, a tall man beside the two red-brown animals. He caught her up and swung her into the air.

"Hurrah, Sally!" he cried. "I shall outgeneral Aunt Nannie. I have at last a campaign."

Sally leaned down serenely and kissed him. She had not seen him in such high spirits since the evening that the letter came during the salt haying. He returned her kiss, and let her slip to the ground, where she stood, feeling the warm breath of the oxen coming and going on her hand.

He sat down on a rock and she sat at his feet, sometimes looking past him to the blue sky where a hawk was whistling.

"It's like this, Sally," he said. "Your Aunt Nannie is not one to be driven, and she's not one to be led either. She knows now it would be best for us all to go, but she would rather die than go back on her spoken word. But how is she to give in? I think I see a way," and he smiled to himself again.

"What shall you do, Uncle Joseph" asked Sally. "Tuggie Noyes said you both would have your wills."

"I'll do my best, I'll do my best," he answered, and Sally saw that he was shaking with silent laughter.

"Oh, tell me, sir, do," begged Sally.

"I've said enough, Sally," said he. "You shall see. But not a word about this to anyone, mind you." And he swung himself to his feet in his swift silent way, laughed again, and called *gee* to his oxen, which had been standing chewing their cuds, and now heaved quietly forward like two slow brown waves.

From that moment Sally watched everything that Uncle Joseph did, eager as a kitten. He hired a man named Jehoshaphat Mountain, and with Uncle Eben's occasional help cut down some large trees and hauled them to the mill to be made into boards. And to help in the work he brought back a team of white oxen, big creamy-colored beasts that seemed beautiful to Sally as they leaned forward straining against their blue yoke.

Then one day Uncle Joseph came back with a pair of black and white oxen.

Sally saw them from the window.

"Uncle Joseph's brought another yoke of oxen!" she called, and the aunts crowded to the window to see.

"An ox is a handsome creature, I always say," said Aunt Esther as she watched them walking up the lane, their broad foreheads swinging.

Aunt Nannie pursed her lips and opened the kitchen door.

"Brother Joseph!" she called sharply as he came near. "What are you going to do with all these cattle?"

Uncle Joseph moved his rod, and the oxen came to a slow halt. He looked at Aunt Nannie mildly, with a glance of hidden amusement.

"It's a sort of speculation," he explained. "I mean to winter five or six yoke. Cheap in the fall, dear in the spring. We had a good harvest this year."

Aunt Nannie returned to her spinning, completely satisfied.

"Brother Joseph always knows how to turn a good penny," said Aunt Deborah admiringly. "There's not his match in the county."

It was the unspoken rule of the household that everything outside the house was in Uncle Joseph's charge, and everything within was in Aunt Nannie's. If Uncle Joseph were building a new shed he would tell them all in good time. But Sally, saying nothing, noticed a good deal. Uncle Joseph no longer took her into the far pasture with him. Uncle Eben chuckled over his "Gazette" and chocolate at tea, and the oxen kept on coming, until the barn was crowded with them.

When all the other leaves are gone
The brown oak leaves still linger on,
Their branches obstinately lifted
To frozen wind and snow deep-drifted.

But when the winter is well passed
The brown oak leaves drop down at last,
To let the little buds appear
No larger than a mouse's ear.

6. *Great-aunt Colman*

"THIS IS no time of the year to be traipsing about visiting, Brother Joseph," said Aunt Nannie one day in late January.

"On the contrary, winter is the best time for visiting," said Uncle Joseph. "It breaks the days indoors. You're looking pale, Nannie, and so are the girls. You haven't been out for a month."

It was true that Aunt Nannie was not her usual bustling red-cheeked self, but whether that was from being indoors or whether it was from the struggle going on inside herself—with one part saying, "Give in, Nannie," and the other part saying, "You said you wouldn't and you stick by your word, Nannie"—who can tell?

In the end, however, she agreed to visit Sally's great-aunt, the widow Colman, in her big house in Quincy. Uncle Joseph had made all the arrangements and Great-aunt Colman was expecting her three nieces and (since it was Saturday) her grand-niece Sally, too, for dinner and the day. Sally was tremendously excited.

"Great-aunt Colman," said Uncle Eben, "is never happy without a parrot, a monkey, and a little negro page. You're sure to find them all there, Sally."

Sally grew so impatient while the aunts were putting on their Sunday best, with their brooches, gold beads, and rings, that she had to run out to the barn to help Uncle Joseph harness Dorcas. It was a mild day with a slight haze in the air. Dorcas was pleased to be going out and whinnied, answered by Uncle Joseph's big horse Peacock, while from both sides of the barn came the patient breathing and stamping of all the oxen and cows.

The aunts were waiting and came rustling out. Aunt Esther was wearing two pairs of mittens since she was to drive. Sally sat on Aunt Deborah's lap, trying to make herself light.

"Good-bye, Brother! Good-bye, Uncle! Good-bye!" and they were off.

The snow was a little soft, and Dorcas's hoofs sent snowballs rattling against the dashboard, while the bells rang out with a gentle wildness. The sun looked small and white in the haze. Although the snow was deep she knew that spring was coming nearer with every day, and soon they would be weaving linen again on the looms in the back chamber, and then would come the dipping of candles and the soap-making, outdoors in the black iron soap caldron. Every month had its special occupations indoors and out, like the little pictures at the top of each page in the almanac that hung beside the chimney.

Dorcas was going more slowly now. The first flush of energy was over and she was settling down to a quiet trot. They were beyond the country that Sally knew. Strange hills and inlets, where the water was gray-purple against the shore-ice, appeared at every turn of the road. Sometimes they met other sleighs and had to jerk out of the comfortable ruts with a jarring of the bells, to let them pass. The journey seemed too short to Sally. In less than an hour and a half they stood at the great white door of Aunt Colman's town house, with Aunt Nannie's hand firmly raising the knocker.

It was the housekeeper, Mrs. Peabody, who opened the door, while a boy took Dorcas to the stable.

There was much curtseying back and forth and polite greetings, and then they were taken into a parlor with a fresh-lit fire on the hearth.

In their own house none of the rooms were papered and the floors were bare except for a small rug in the best parlor, but here the walls were hung with a fine French paper, showing scenes from the seasons, the draperies at the windows were of heavy velvet, and there were rugs covering all the floor, and on the tables were silver candlesticks. Overhead Sally could hear the sharp jangling of a bell and much hurrying to and fro of feet. Her aunts made a little conversation, bringing out their go-abroad sewing and settling their skirts.

Then the door flung open and a little negro page appeared with a low bow, ushering in Great-aunt Colman, who entered leaning on Mrs. Peabody's arm. She looked like Aunt Nannie, but much older, redder, and crosser. She had on a white wrapper, and over her gray curls was a great black crape turban, and there were red velvet slippers on her feet, and a gold-headed cane in her hand. Mrs. Peabody carried a fan and a scent bottle, and behind came a young maid with a shawl and cushions and a foot-stool.

Sally and her aunts immediately rose and curtseyed at her entrance, but except for a light nod Great-aunt Colman was much too busy to pay any attention to her nieces. She tried this chair and then that. Now she would sit by the window; but no, it was draughty, she would try the couch by the fire. The cushions were never right.

Then the door flung open and a little negro page appeared with a low bow, ushering in Great-aunt Colman.

"There, child, put the stool under my feet, not under the chair. Mrs. Peabody, the shawl is choking me, I do declare!"

But at last she was comfortably settled and reached for her scent bottle and her fan. With a few sniffs of one and a few waves of the other she was enough recovered to turn to her nieces.

"How do you do, Nannie? Deborah, you are as much of a mouse as ever, I see. But, Esther, I hear you're like to be a bride. Sally, child, come near and let me see you. No, leave off your curtseying. You take after your mother and will be as pretty, too. No, Nannie, don't shake your head. Let her know it. There are enough ugly things in the world."

The day was one of enchantment for Sally. The page and the young maid brought in honey-wine and fruit cake, always served to guests, and later at their mistress's order they came in with a monkey named Jackanapes, and Turk, a big parrot on an ebony stand. Sally was afraid of them both.

"And well you may be, child," said her great-aunt with satisfaction. "They are both as ill-natured as may be and would sooner bite than eat." But they were full of amusing tricks, too, and when they were taken out of the parlor Sally asked permission to go with them, and soon grew familiar enough to roll an apple with Jackanapes.

They came in with a monkey named Jackanapes,
and Turk, a big parrot on an ebony stand.

Dinner was such a meal as Sally had never seen, though Great-aunt Colman apologized for not making company of them. Sally marveled that one woman could eat so much every day of the year, but she tasted the delicacies herself with relish, trying to remember each one to describe to Uncle Eben when she should be at home again.

"What pretty china, my dear Aunt," said Aunt Nannie.

"Crown Derby, just imported from London," said Great-aunt Colman, looking at it proudly.

After dinner they were taken into another parlor as grand as the first, with a glass chandelier hanging from the ceiling like a bouquet of icicles, and in one corner a spinet inlaid with mother-of-pearl flowers.

"This may be your last visit here for some time," said Great-aunt Colman. "Mrs. Peabody, pray bring me my jewel-case. I should like to give Miss Sally a keepsake to remember her Great-aunt by."

"But we are going nowhere, Aunt," said Aunt Nannie, a little breathlessly.

"Stuff and nonsense, child!" returned Aunt Colman, tapping the floor with her gold-headed stick. "Of course you're going. Where have you got to, in all these years? Give Joseph a fair chance and you may fold your hands and rest when you're my age."

Mrs. Peabody came back into the room with a large jewel-case in her hands and a gold key. She brought a small table beside Great-aunt Colman's chair, and put the case upon it.

Great-aunt Colman opened it and brought out brooches, rings, necklaces, bracelets, and ear-drops; but for each it was, "No, no, that is not suitable"—or, "I could never bring myself to part with that!" The case was almost empty, and it looked as though Great-aunt Colman had asked for her jewels more to display them than to give them away. Sally watched, fascinated. She had never known there was so much jewelry in the world.

The crape turban shook.

"I'm afraid there is nothing here for you, child," said Great-aunt Colman. But Sally was scarcely disappointed. All these things seemed too grand to belong to her world.

Mrs. Peabody, still standing beside her mistress, reached forward and brought out from the bottom of the case a little chain of round coral beads alternating with gold ones.

"Would this be what Madam Colman is looking for?" she asked.

Great-aunt Colman gave her a cross look, to which Mrs. Peabody paid no attention.

"It is too small for Madam Colman," she went on. "You

have not been able to wear it for ten years." Her voice was quiet and matter-of-fact.

"I suppose, Sally, you may as well have it," said Great-aunt Colman shortly, but Mrs. Peabody gave Sally a quick, kind smile. It was the only time during the day that she had taken any part in the conversation, but one could see that she had more power in the household than at first appeared.

Sally, blushing and happy, thanked her great-aunt and fastened the little gold clasp, shaped like a hand, behind her neck. The beads were small and gay. She loved them.

Soon afterwards they took their departure.

"Brother Joseph was most anxious that we should be back for tea," explained Aunt Nannie.

"I shall have my afternoon sleep, then," said Great-aunt Colman, brightening. "I have enjoyed seeing you, my dears, and may you have a pleasant journey."

"But—" began Aunt Nannie.

"Pish!" interrupted Great-aunt Colman, taking Mrs. Peabody's arm and leading the way to the door. There she gave them each a dry pecking kiss like a parrot's, and everyone else curtseyed, and Sally had a last glimpse of the little negro's woolly head and wide eyes as he closed the white door.

The earth is lighter
Than the sky,
The world is wider
Than in spring,
Along white roads
The sleighs go by,
Icily sweet
The sleigh-bells ring.

The birds are gone
Into the south,
The leaves are fallen
To the ground;
But singing shakes
Each sleigh-bell's mouth,
And leaf-like ears
Turn towards the sound.

7. *Aunt Nannie's House*

THEY DROVE home quickly. When Dorcas stopped at the back door it was still light, but there was no sign of the uncles, or of Jehoshaphat Mountain. Then, as Sally started to take the mare to the barn, she was stopped by several voices coming down the wood-road, men's voices gee-hawing oxen, and the screech of heavy runners on snow. The three aunts paused on the doorstep and Sally jumped from the sleigh to watch, as out of the darkness of the last pine thicket appeared the strangest thing she had ever seen. First came Peacock, Uncle Joseph's big horse, with Uncle Joseph on his back, and then six yoke of oxen, led by the red pair from their own farm, treading through the heavy snow in a slow procession of swaying heads and thick necks. Beside them walked Uncle Eben and Jehoshaphat Mountain with long poles, and behind them—wonder of wonders!—came a little house on runners, a house with windows whose small panes sparkled in the late light, with a doorstep, and a water-barrel under the drip of the roof, and a chimney pipe from which smoke was actually rising.

Sally jumped up and down, clapping her mittened hands, Aunt Esther uttered a cry of delight, and Uncle Joseph stood up in his stirrups and waved. But Aunt Nannie made no motion, and uttered no sound.

Slowly the line drew to the step and stopped.

"Nannie," said Uncle Joseph in a solemn voice, "here is a house I have built for you and which I give you with all my heart, so that you may travel to the district of Maine and yet never leave your own fire."

He paused and they all waited, Peacock pawing the snow.

But Aunt Nannie's face was still blank with surprise, and did not show her thoughts. She felt behind her for the door to support herself, and once she tried to speak but could not. In the long silence Sally heard her own heart pounding like a colt galloping over a frozen meadow.

"Thank you, Brother Joseph," said Aunt Nannie at last in a small gentle voice, "thank you, my dear, I shall go willingly."

And behind them—wonder of wonders!
—came a little house on runners.

Sally let her breath out in a gasp of joy, and Uncle Joseph jumped from the saddle and kissed Aunt Nannie, who cried a little, mostly from relief because he had made it easy for her to give in and yet keep her word.

"Dorcas will take herself to the barn, Sally," Uncle Joseph called. "Come and see Aunt Nannie's house," and they all crowded in together. It was small, of course, but bright with windows, and warm with the Franklin stove which had a little fire burning in it. Two big beds stood in two corners of the room, covered with the blue eagle woven quilts. There was a smooth wooden sink and several chairs, and china in racks on the walls. Behind the larger room was a small room with two bunks in it for the uncles.

"There will be sleds for the rest of the furniture, Nannie," went on Uncle Joseph. "I have hired some men and their teams from down the road. You will, I imagine, wish to take our own cows, and Dorcas and the sleigh will bring up the rear, so that you may all take an airing when you grow tired of being in the house. And here, Deborah, are your seeds for a new garden, and we will carry some of your bulbs and roots on the sleds."

"And Aunt Esther will be a bride before the leaves turn yellow in Tuggie Noyes' woods!" cried Sally.

"Sally!" protested Aunt Esther laughing a little.

"I may come back and fetch someone to take your place, if it's not too much trouble," said Uncle Eben.

"Eliza is worth a good deal more trouble than that, Brother Sit-by-the-fire!" exclaimed Aunt Esther indignantly.

"How soon do we flit, Brother Joseph?" Aunt Nannie asked as she hung up her cloak on a peg and seated herself in her own chair, taking out her go-abroad sewing which she had brought back with her from Great-aunt Colman's.

"It's a picture to see you," said Uncle Joseph, smiling at her. They looked at each other and made their peace without a word being spoken. "I wanted this to be a surprise for you like the doll's house I made when you were a little girl. That's why I packed you all off to Quincy to have you out of the way while we furnished the house. But you asked when we would leave, Nannie. In a week, if you can be ready, my dear, so that we may have the advantage of the snow. The neighbors will help you."

"It doesn't matter what else you take," said Uncle Eben, "so long as you have plenty of meat-pies and apple-pies, baked beans, doughnuts, chocolate cake, pound cake, roasted chickens, hams—"

"Here, here," said Aunt Deborah, affectionately putting a hand across his lips, "you must not sound so greedy, Brother." She took her hand quickly away, for he had nipped it.

"Only a nibble," he joked her. "I've always said you had a sweet hand, Debby."

Meantime Jehoshaphat Mountain had been unyoking the oxen and taking them yoke by yoke to their quarters in the barn.

"I've been building the house for weeks in the wood lot," went on Uncle Joseph. "'Twill be a good way to carry our goods and ourselves without having to put up at the ordinaries, which they say are sometimes poor and dirty. And when we reach our land we shall have this to live in until we can build better. A new home, Nannie, on wider acres."

It was Sally who discovered the six little pots steaming in the rack that had been made for them on the stove. Uncle Eben, always ready to help in any matter of food, showed Sally where a pine table let down from the wall. She found the cloth and silver spoons and a jar of cookies, and soon six cups were filled, Uncle Joseph's with coffee, Uncle Eben's with chocolate, Aunt Nannie's with old Hyson, Aunt Deborah's with new Hyson, Aunt

Esther's with Souchong, and Sally's with milk and chocolate. And so they shared their first meal in the house that was to carry them to a new land.

Swift things are beautiful:
Swallows and deer,
And lightning that falls
Bright-veined and clear,
Rivers and meteors,
Wind in the wheat,
The strong-withered horse,
The runner's sure feet.

And slow things are beautiful:
The closing of day,
The pause of the wave
That curves downward to spray,
The ember that crumbles,
The opening flower,
And the ox that moves on
In the quiet of power.

8. *The Start*

UNCLE JOSEPH rode Peacock to the head of the procession, a dark figure in the early dawn. The men shouted, the oxen strained, and the little house shivered, then jerked forward with a screeching of runners, and the long journey was begun.

"They're off!" shouted Captain Dagget, waving his red muffler.

"They're off!" cried old Mrs. Captain Dagget, her white kerchief thrashing up and down in her mittened hand.

"Hip, hip, hurrah!" piped little John Hale from Sweet Brook Farm, running beside the oxen, waving his stocking cap.

"Good-bye, good-bye! Write me, my dearest Esther!" called Mrs. Caleb, beginning to cry.

All the neighbors were gathered at the doorstep to see them go, although the sun had not yet fully risen, and the snow seemed dark and grave against the pale yellow sky.

Sally stood in the doorway of the little house in her red cloak, with her aunts behind her. She could see the broad strong backs of the twelve oxen straining as they started on their road, and beyond them rose the farm-house, the only home she had ever known. It looked so low and strong, with its wide chimney and a dark sparkle on the little panes of glass in the windows, and their friends standing on the doorstep! Her cheeks stung with cold and tears, and she felt suddenly a great hollow inside her. Then they came to the road and Uncle Joseph turned in his saddle and waved to her. Peacock was pulling at the bit, prancing, impatient to be off.

"To Maine!" called Uncle Joseph, making a gesture northward. "To Maine!"

The oxen quickened their pace on the beaten highway. Jehoshaphat Mountain shouted cheerfully at them. The sunlight caught the tops of the trees and the church weathervane in the distance. Sally heard a cow low behind her and knew it was old Brindle.

"We're off! We're off!" she thought, her mind turning to the future. "At last, we're off!"

"Come in, child, and shut the door," said Aunt Nannie,

and Sally came in. Did ever a little girl go traveling like this before, in a doll's house on runners, seeing everything go by! She hung up her cloak and sat looking out of one of the little windows, watching how astonished people looked at seeing them. Whenever she waved, she did it stiffly, and she pretended she couldn't move her head at all.

"What *is* the matter, Sally?" asked Aunt Deborah, looking up from her sewing. "Have you caught rheumatism, child?"

"No, I'm being a doll," said Sally. "We're all dolls and this is our home."

Aunt Esther jumped up and did a doll's dance. Her eyes were shining, her curls bobbed up and down. Even Aunt Nannie smiled above the stocking she was knitting.

"Now, have we forgotten anything?" asked Aunt Deborah. "Where's Dinah's basket?"

Dinah was the black cat. She was shiny black all over, except for her paws and a star in the hollow of her throat, and a little white chin that always made her look as though she had just been drinking milk.

"Dinah, Dinah," called Sally.

"Mew," said Dinah, answering dismally from under one of the big beds.

Sally got down on her knees and pulled out the covered basket in which Dinah was imprisoned. When she took the cover off, Dinah jumped out, but she paid no attention to any of her mistresses. Round and round the room she went, with her nose extended, smelling everything, her tail stiff, her ears a little flattened. She smelled the pipe from the sink, she went into the corners, she disappeared under the beds, she sniffed at the furniture. She pushed open the door into the little room and investigated that. Then when she had thoroughly looked over every inch of this new home, she exclaimed, "Prrr!," stopped looking wary, and neatly jumped onto one of the beds, in the exact spot where the sunlight from the south window met the warmth of the stove. Kneading the place for a moment with her little white paws to make sure that it was soft, she turned round once, and went to sleep, as though traveling to Maine were something she had done all her life.

"Well, I declare, Dinah," said Aunt Nannie, "you *do* know how to make yourself comfortable! I suppose with all of us cooped up here together you'd best go where you've a mind to, but once in Maine I'll thank you to keep off the beds."

Getting dinner was great fun.

"We can't all be turning round in here like a lot of tops," said Aunt Nannie. "Deborah, you and Esther sit where you are and Sally and I will get things ready."

Sally gave her aunt a grateful look. And Aunt Nannie's ear-drops jingled back at her as Aunt Nannie nodded. They both had to learn to fit their walking to the movement of the house, especially when it jerked over a rut, but soon the potatoes were poked deep into the ashes, and the little table was laid with dishes taken down from the wall. Sally hung onto the doorstep while she dipped water from the barrel outside, breaking the thin skim of ice across it. It felt good outdoors in the cold, sunny air with the oxen pulling solemnly at their yokes and Peacock settled down to a slow walk, and the caw of a crow and the creak of snow for sound. Sally jumped down and ran along beside Jehoshaphat Mountain. An ox rolled his eyes at her, and she put her hand on his spotted white shoulder. It felt warm and muscular to her touch.

At noon they pulled the house to one side of the road, and all the horses and cattle were given feed. The hired men built a fire and ate around it, but Uncle Joseph and Uncle Eben had their dinner in the little house.

"There's no room for me at the table," said Uncle Eben, "but I know where the warmest place in the room is.

Scat, Dinah!" And he made himself comfortable where she had been. Dinah blinked her yellow eyes at him, stood up, stretched one leg after another, yawned so that her pink tongue showed stiff and curly, and then lay down again out of his way farther up on the bed.

"Dinah and I understand each other," said Uncle Eben, scratching her under the chin. "Don't we, Dinah?"

Dinah caught his finger between her two front paws and pretended to bite it, purring in gusts which, with her mouth open, sounded almost like growls.

"Careful, old girl," said Uncle Eben. "You must set an example of good behavior to all the cats in Maine."

That evening they stopped at a farm on the outskirts of Boston where they could find shelter for their animals in the big barn. The teamsters slept in the loft, but Sally and her family made themselves snug in the little house. It was drawn up in a barnyard, across which Sally could see the lighted kitchen windows of the farm, and the dim outlines of its roofs. A man came to see them, holding a lantern, but it was too late for visiting. By candlelight they had their supper of bread and cheese and warm milk just drawn from the cows.

"Twelve miles—a good journey for the first day," said Uncle Joseph, contentedly, after supper. "And now to bed, for we must be up early in the morning."

"Read us first the promise to Joseph, Brother Joseph," said Aunt Deborah, and Sally jumped up and brought the heavy Bible from its box and laid it on Uncle Joseph's knees. He drew the candle near and, after thumbing the pages until he found the place, read in his warm quiet voice:

"'Blessed of the Lord be his land, for the precious things of heaven, for the dew, and for the deep that coucheth beneath, and for the precious fruits brought forth by the sun, and for the precious things put forth by the moon, and for the chief things of the ancient mountains, and for the precious things of the lasting hills, and for the precious things of the earth and the fulness thereof—'"

"That is God's blessing upon farmers," said Aunt Nannie.

"It makes me feel warm inside," whispered Sally to Aunt Esther. And then when the uncles had gone into the back room, they all raced one another to bed. Aunt Nannie and Aunt Deborah shared one bed, Aunt Esther and Sally the other. It was Sally who jumped in first, and she was asleep almost as soon as the blankets were under her chin. But once in the night she woke up to find the room growing cold and Dinah beside her—the cat had jumped up and now, rubbing against her cheek before she slipped in under the clothes, she curled up against Sally's chest, her black head on the pillow beside her mistress's.

THE START

Out of the dark
To the sill of the door
Lay the snow in a long
Unruffled floor,
And the candlelight fell
Narrow and thin,
A carpet unrolled
For the cat to walk in.
Slowly, smoothly,
Black as the night,
With paws unseen,
White upon white,
Like a queen who walks
Down a corridor,
The black cat paced
The cold smooth floor,
And left behind her
Bead upon bead
The track of small feet
Like dark fernseed.

9. *The Portrait*

THE EVENING they reached the Kennebec River it had been thawing all day. The oxen had to pull hard, and the little house jolted and jerked over the rocks sticking through the melting ruts.

"Good gracious," exclaimed Aunt Nannie as she pricked her finger with her needle, "I declare Brother Joseph should know better!"

The dishes rattled so on the walls that even Dinah's naps were disturbed. Finally, she gave up trying to go to sleep at all and sat up looking indignant and washed herself instead. She seemed so cross that Sally broke out laughing. Dinah gave her one look, and disappeared out of sight.

When the beds were made and the dishes washed and the little floor brushed and tidy, Sally put on her red cloak and went out. Clear water was running down the ruts, and there was a sweet cold smell in the air. Walking be-

side the oxen was hard, for her feet slipped, and soon Uncle Joseph swung her up behind him on Peacock's back, and she rode holding onto his coat, at the head of the procession. The country was wilder than any she had known. The road ran between walls of forest, towering and thick, not held back by the stone walls to which she had always been accustomed.

"Look," said Uncle Joseph, and peeping around his back she saw a buck and two does standing in the road watching their approach. Now and then they passed cleared land and farms, where the people ran to the doors to wave to them as they went by. Sally waved back gaily, but no one had eyes for anything but the little house, jolting and jerking behind the oxen. In spite of the bad going, they traveled far that day, struggling on until after dark to reach the tavern at the Kennebec Ferry. By the time she saw the lights shining cheerfully from its windows, Sally was so sleepy that she was glad to slip into bed, and knew nothing more but a vague sound of men and cattle passing beyond the wall of their go-abroad dwelling.

But in the morning there was much excitement.

"Wouldn't trust that ice just now if I was in your boots," said the ferryman. "Better wait a day or two until she's froze solid again. It's only fit for cats after that thaw."

The weather was already colder and Uncle Joseph had to agree, after riding Peacock a little way out on the river and seeing the flaws and ice pools just beginning to skim over.

"Never mind," said Aunt Nannie cheerfully, jingling her ear-drops. "I needed to bake some more bread, and here's my opportunity."

"Pies, too," said Uncle Eben. "Don't fret, Joseph—Maine isn't going to run away while our backs are turned."

After breakfast Sally's aunts all went to the tavern to ask permission to do their baking and washing. Even Dinah jumped daintily out into the snow and, making sure that the tavern dog was really chained, began exploring the barn for rats. Sally stayed behind for a little to make the house neat, and then picked her way across the yard. A white-haired woman, standing straight and tall, opened the door when she knocked.

"Come in, my dear," she said with a sudden warm smile. "You are welcome as sunshine."

"Thank you, ma'am," said Sally, curtseying and smiling back.

"Put your cloak on the peg, child," said the woman. "Your aunts and I are busy but perhaps you will call on my son. He's never busy if there's a child in the house. You'll find him in the north chamber, my dear."

Sally knocked at the north chamber door. A man's voice said, "Come in," and she stepped inside and stopped. Such a room she had never seen. All the walls and furniture were covered with pictures; and in the middle stood a blue-eyed young man looking at her with cheerful friendliness. He was painting a large picture of a man in a blue coat with brass buttons, a telescope in his hand, and a ship in the background.

"But he hasn't any head, sir," said Sally gazing.

"We'll get him a head next summer, my dear," said the young man. "In June I harness Merrylegs and we go out and find people willing to buy my pictures if I paint in their own heads. I'll show you how it's done."

Sally sat very still, watching the young man's busy hands.

And in a moment he had gone over to the wall and from a heap of pictures selected one and held it out to her. It was of a little girl in a white dress with green ribbons and a parrakeet perched on her hand.

"This is just the thing," he said. "Will you oblige me, child, by sitting in the chair there over beyond the window, and looking at me? Pretend you are at meeting, my dear, and sit still."

Sally had never had such a morning. Looking at her with a bright darting glance, the young man stood painting and talking. But all the time he talked he worked, and when Aunt Nannie's voice was heard calling below he put his finger to his lips.

"Not a word to anyone," he whispered. "Come back after dinner."

So after dinner Sally again tapped at his door. This time she had brought Dinah with her, thinking the cat would like to sit on the hearth; and Dinah did, though for some time she was busy cleaning off her nose which she had foolishly covered with paint while sniffing at the portrait of the sailor leaning against the wall. It gave her a fit of sneezing in which she almost shook off her whiskers.

But fortunately the painter cleaned her with a paint rag, and soon she folded her paws before the fire and purred herself to sleep. Sally sat very still, watching the young man's busy hands and the light slowly dying out of the room.

At last, when it was almost dark and she was growing stiff, he gave a sigh and said, "There, it's done!" and Sally jumped up and ran to see it. Yes, it was Sally that looked back at her—black-curled, black-eyed, with lips just ready to smile, but Sally in ribbons, Sally with a parrakeet, Sally out of a storybook.

"Dinah, look at that!" she cried, picking Dinah up in her arms and showing her the picture. Dinah yawned and looked away.

"You're jealous," said Sally, laughing. "Oh, please, sir, may I tell them, now? Aunt Nannie may shake her head, but Aunt Deborah will love to see it, and so will the others."

"It's yours, my dear," said the young man bowing. "It's St. Valentine's Day, you know, and this is a Valentine's gift to the prettiest lady who ever sat to me."

Sally drew his head down and kissed him. People were the nicest part of all the adventure, she thought in a sudden moment of insight. It wasn't just moving on—it was the meetings that counted.

And that was how it happened that a portrait of Sally hung on the walls of the go-abroad house when two days later it left the tavern and creaked and slid its way safely across the ice of the Kennebec River.

THE RABBITS' SONG OUTSIDE THE TAVERN

We, who play under the pines,
We, who dance in the snow
That shines blue in the light of the moon,
Sometimes halt as we go—
Stand with our ears erect,
Our noses testing the air,
To gaze at the golden world
Behind the windows there.

Suns they have in a cave,
Stars, each on a tall white stem,
And the thought of a fox or an owl
Seems never to trouble them.
They laugh and eat and are warm,
Their food is ready at hand,
While hungry out in the cold
We little rabbits stand.

But they never dance as we dance!
They haven't the speed nor the grace.
We scorn both the dog and the cat
Who lie by their fireplace.
We scorn them licking their paws
Their eyes on an upraised spoon—
We who dance hungry and wild
Under a winter's moon.

10. *The Cub*

WILDER AND wilder grew the country through which they passed, and farther and farther apart were the settlements, but still the little house went on. One day when Dinah was running along beside the oxen, as she sometimes liked to do for a little while, she was almost carried away by a fox that chased her right in among the oxen's hoofs before sliding off into the woods again like a red shadow. After that, Sally never let Dinah down without walking with her, and Dinah herself kept looking over her black shoulders at the woods.

Sometimes they made long journeys and sometimes short, for it was not so easy now to make sure that the cattle had a barn-roof over them each night.

One morning Sally was walking by herself at the head of the procession. A feeling of early spring was in her bones. They had passed some men sugaring off, boiling the maple syrup in big kettles over a leaping fire, sunk deep in the snow. The men called out to them and came to admire the little house and look over the oxen. They insisted that the ladies must take a crock of their syrup and would accept no pay.

"You'll do as much for us some time," said one of them.

Sally walked on, eating a piece of bread and syrup carefully, her eyes on a scolding squirrel in one of the trees. When she looked ahead she saw someone or something coming towards them. For a long time she thought it must be a man with a dog, but when they came nearer she saw that the animal was a black bear-cub on a chain. The little bear shambled along, swinging his head from side to side. His coat was black and shiny except about his nose which was brown. His little eyes looked at her expectantly. When the man who was leading him stopped, the cub sat down and held the chain between his front paws like clumsy hands.

"How do you do?" said Sally, looking from the cub to the man who was with him. He was an Indian, tall and thin, wearing an old coat and hat that had belonged to white men, but his leggings and moccasins were made of fringed buckskin. He smiled at her gravely and she smiled back. She had seen few Indians, but she like them. She put her hand on the cub's head and he dropped the chain and played with her wrists instead.

Uncle Joseph rode up and pulled in Peacock, who snorted. The oxen stopped, heads low, stamping at the smell of wild life.

"He's a real cute little fellow," said Jehoshaphat Mountain, rubbing the bear's ribs with the end of his pole.

"I wish I could have him, Uncle," said Sally wistfully.

"What would you do when he grew big and cross?" asked Uncle Joseph.

"Let him go back to the woods," said Sally.

"I won't have a dratted bear in the house," called Aunt Nannie from the door. "There's enough of us as it is without cubs, I should think."

Uncle Eben had come up.

"Just what I need to keep me warm in the sleigh," he said without a twinkle. "I've been wanting a bear-cub for ever and ever so long. Dinah's too small to be any good as a warmer, and Sally keeps in front of the procession. How much, hey?" he went on to the Indian, and in five minutes he had bought the little bear—collar, chain and all—and carried him off to Dorcas and the sleigh, while Aunt Nannie, and Aunt Deborah, and Aunt Esther crowded to the window to watch.

Dorcas soon got used to the smell of bear, though at first she tried to run away, and from that time on Sally spent a good many hours with Uncle Eben in the sleigh. Hannibal, as the little bear was called, was very fond of

Sally and would cuddle close to her and lick her cheek. He and Uncle Eben talked together, Hannibal in grunts and whines and Uncle Eben pretending to understand and answer.

"You say it's late, do you, and time to have dinner? Well, you'll just have to wait. You don't like waiting, you say? Well, here's a doughnut Sally will give you if you're polite. Now say, 'Thank you.' You won't? And why not? You say one doughnut isn't enough, do you?"

"How can you tell what he's saying, Uncle Eben?" Sally would ask.

"Why, can't *you?*" Uncle Eben seemed surprised. And after a while Sally almost thought she could understand, too.

It took only a few days for the oxen and horses to get

used to having Hannibal near them, but the cows never got over lowering their horns at him when he came close. He usually slept beside Jehoshaphat Mountain in one of the barns at night, but it was Sally who gave him warm milk in the morning and the evening at milking time.

One gray afternoon she and the aunts were sitting in Aunt Nannie's house sewing when Aunt Deborah sighed.

"This afternoon seems long," she said. Through the windows endless trees moved slowly by, each tree making room for another tree to take its place. A little snow was falling.

"Let's invite Hannibal for tea," said Aunt Esther.

Aunt Nannie started to protest, but stopped herself. She thought for a moment and then said to Sally:

"Put on your cloak, child, and tell Master Hannibal that Mrs. Dinah would be honored if he would take a dish of milk with her by the stove."

Uncle Eben pretended to grumble.

"Who's going to keep me warm? What's that you say, you rascal? You don't care? You want to go, anyhow? You've never been introduced to Mrs. Dinah, but you've admired her from a distance? Well, go along, then. I suppose I can keep myself warm," and he pulled Dorcas to a halt while Hannibal scrambled to the ground and Sally and he ran off to the house together.

It was the merriest afternoon. The squirrels in the dark trees at the sides of the road and the few crows passing overhead must have been surprised at the peals of laughter ringing out from the go-abroad house. Even the oxen twitched back their stolid ears to listen, and Peacock pranced as he led the cavalcade. In the first place, Dinah looked furious at having another animal come into her world. She backed slowly towards one of the beds, her back up, her tail like a bottle brush, her ears laid close to her head and her eyes sparkling. When she backed into the bed, she thought something had attacked her from behind and spit like a perfect fury. All the time Hannibal stood looking at her, apologetic and worried, until she went out of sight under the bed. Then the cub saluted each of the ladies, as Uncle Eben had taught him, and Sally brought him an apple. From time to time volleys of hisses came from under the bed to remind them that Dinah was still on hand. Sally had to crawl in after her and bring her out by the scruff of the neck, but after coaxing she finally settled down. When Hannibal's back was turned to her, she crept up softly and patted him with her paw. When he swung around, she retreated hissing, but before an hour was up they were lapping milk out of the same saucer, and by the time the uncles came in for tea Dinah was asleep on Hannibal's shoulder, her head almost lost in his warm fur.

"How do you like my bear, Nannie?" asked Uncle Eben, smacking his lips over his chocolate.

"He's a nice enough little creature," said Aunt Nannie, and then, feeling that she had relented too far, she added quickly, "But what good is he to anyone?"

"You wait and see," said Uncle Eben, more wisely than he knew, for it was not many days before Hannibal proved his usefulness in a very unexpected way.

"Who are *you?*" asked the cat of the bear.
"I am a child of the wood,
I am strong with rain-shedding hair,
I hunt without fear for my food,
The others behold me and quail."
Said the cat, "You are lacking a tail."

"What can you *do?*" asked the cat.
"I can climb for the honey I crave.
In the fall when I'm merry and fat
I seek out a suitable cave
And sleep till I feel the spring light."
Said the cat, "Can you see in the night?"

Said the cat, "*I* sit by man's fire,
But I am much wilder than you.
I do the thing I desire
And do nothing I don't want to do.
I am small, but then, what is that?
My spirit is great," said the cat.

11. *The Storm*

"I DON'T like the feel of the air," said Aunt Deborah timidly one morning as they were having breakfast.

"What's wrong with it, Debby?" asked Uncle Eben helping himself to another piece of pie.

"It feels like a storm," said Aunt Deborah shivering. "I wish, Brother Joseph, you would put up here for another day."

Sally looked from the window and saw the men bringing the cattle out of the crude log barn in which they had been crowded together the night before. Beyond them she saw the settler's cabin, an untidy sort of place in a clearing ugly with raw stumps sticking through the snow. They were so near the Penobscot now that she hated the idea of any delay. Aunt Esther hated it, too, Sally could see.

"Better safe than sorry," Aunt Nannie remarked.

"I don't notice anything unusual," said Uncle Joseph. "The wind's northwest and we might get a squall, but nothing to speak of. I'll talk to the man here and see what he says."

Sally watched him consulting with a small bearded man in a raccoon-skin cap. They looked at the sky, wet their fingers and tested the wind. She was glad to see that the yoking of the oxen went on.

"He thinks it's all right, Deborah," said Uncle Joseph, sticking his head through the door, and was off.

Sally loved the start in the morning. All the animals knew now what was expected of them, even Hannibal who clambered into the sleigh by himself and sat among the fur rugs watching everyone with a funny look of pride on his face. Dinah jumped on Sally's lap and looked out, too. Like all cats she was full of curiosity. Then came the fine moment of the morning when Uncle Joseph rode Peacock to the head of the line. Jehoshaphat Mountain and the other men shouted, the oxen heaved forward, the little house gave a lurch as it broke out of its position, and the caravan was off.

The jolt upset Dinah, who retired with a look of irritation for another nap. There was nothing unusual, except that Aunt Deborah still had a worried air. Now they were out of the clearing and in the woods again, going down the narrow rough road between the two endless dark walls of trunks. It was almost dinner time when the snow began. At first it came lightly, and Uncle Eben joked Aunt Deborah, as they ate about the little table.

"Here's your blizzard, Debby," he said affectionately. "Someone's been shaking a feather-bed somewhere."

But Uncle Joseph did not joke. He hurried through his meal, and soon Sally saw him helping to get the oxen in line again. In half the usual time they were on the road, with Jehoshaphat urging on the teams to their greatest speed. The snow fell heavier and heavier, and now most of the windows were covered thick with it and the little house was dark. Sally, peering through the sheltered top of a window, could no longer see the leaders, but only the backs of the nearest pair.

Aunt Deborah lit the lamp in silence, and the aunts knitted quietly together. Sally went to put a stick of wood on the fire.

"No, child," said Aunt Nannie, looking up. "We had better save the wood."

Sally sat by the window on the lee side staring out, but she could not see two feet ahead of her. Several times she had a shadowy glimpse of Uncle Joseph riding by on Peacock. Once he tapped on the window, and leaned out of the saddle so that his face was near the glass. He looked at her inquiringly, his hair and eyebrows matted with snow. Sally wanted to cry, but she smiled and nodded at him instead. All was well in the house. He disappeared again into the curtain of snow.

Dinah lay in Sally's lap, but though Sally stroked and coaxed her, she would not purr. Sometimes she shivered and burrowed her head against Sally as though she were trying to get away from something. The room was growing colder, and all the time it seemed to Sally that the little house was going more and more slowly. Sometimes it stopped, and she knew an ox had stumbled, but always it went on again.

"Put the stick on now, child," said Aunt Nannie from the silence. "The fire mustn't go out."

"I wish we'd followed your advice, Aunt Deborah," said Sally, as she put a small stick on the embers.

"Tut, my dear," answered Aunt Deborah almost sharply. "There's no use crying over spilled milk."

"Do you think Uncle Eben and Hannibal are safe?" whispered Sally, voicing the fear that had been in her mind for a long time now.

"Of course," said Aunt Nannie, "or Brother Joseph wouldn't go on. But I wish I felt so sure of old Brindle and the cows."

Then there was silence again—only the knitting needles and the clock sounded in the room, and outside the snow fell and fell, and the wearying oxen stumbled forward through the deepening drifts, and the little house still crept slowly onward towards the Penobscot.

It was Dinah who first gave the signal that the storm was over. She jumped down from Sally's lap, yawned, and began washing her paws. Sally, who had been in a sort of trance, looked out and then clapped her hands.

"I can see the trees, Aunt Nannie! Look, Aunt Deborah! Look, Aunt Esther, there are the trees again!" It seemed to her like heaven, just to see the forest beside the road, after the blinding hours they had been through.

The snow was over as quickly as it had come. In another half-hour the last flurry had fallen, and Sally in her red cloak, under a clearing sky, was floundering in the deep drifts, making her way back to Uncle Eben.

"Are the cows all there?" she called to one of the men.

He wiped his mitten across his face and grinned, nodding. The cows were plodding on, their sides heaving with the effort, but the oxen ahead had trampled the path for them and the little house had broken part of the force of the storm.

"Hello!" said a cheerful voice, and, looking up, all her fear melted into one peal of laughter. Two white snow-crusted faces surrounded by snowy fur were turned to her from the sleigh, two pairs of brown eyes looked at her kindly, two fat bodies in bearskins sat side by side.

"I can't tell which is which," Sally said, "but may I come up?"

The bells stopped ringing. In a moment she was tucked in under the rugs between the other two and the sleigh-bells returned to their gay wild song. All the time the caravan moved on.

"It wouldn't be safe to let the beasts stand," explained Uncle Eben. "Joseph will keep them moving so they won't stiffen. Easy does it. There's nothing to worry about now."

He beat his mittened hands against his chest.

"Don't you want to come in and get warm, Uncle Eben?" asked Sally anxiously.

"Can't desert the ship," said Uncle Eben. "Don't worry, my dear, I'm right as rain. But you might take Hannibal in to warm his nose. He hasn't any hair on it, you know."

The world seemed beautiful as Sally and Hannibal made their way forward towards the house. The road

Two white snow-crusted faces surrounded by snowy fur.

was soft and white as the breasts of pigeons, and the dark pine branches were bending under heavy epaulettes of snow. Here and there a birch was doubled almost into an arch, and the thickets were mounded whitenesses. A cow lowed, a man shouted, the sleigh-bells rang cheerfully, and Sally and Hannibal made slow haste through this ermine world to overtake the house moving slowly ahead.

But suddenly Hannibal was pulling sideways at his chain.

"Hurry up," cried Sally, giving it a jerk.

But Hannibal refused to budge.

He had his little beady eyes fixed on something by the side of the road which Sally had not noticed. It looked like a log, almost hidden with snow, which some woodcutter had left leaning against a pine.

Sally's feet were cold.

"Don't be silly, Hannibal," she exclaimed, tugging with all her might.

But Hannibal would not come. Instead, he began pulling Sally towards the log.

"Drat the bear!" thought Sally to herself, but she had to give in. Better let Hannibal get his idea out of his head, whatever it was. She wondered if there could be a honey tree near by. Here the snow was unbroken, but she managed to struggle after Hannibal.

"What's up?" called Uncle Eben, stopping Dorcas.

"It's Hannibal," Sally called back. "I can't do anything with him."

They had almost reached the stump, and the cub turned and looked at her as though saying, "There, do you see now?"

And Sally, looking closely, did see at last.

"Uncle Eben!" she called. "Oh, Uncle Eben! It's a man!"

"Oh, Uncle Eben! It's a man!"

Cold winter now is in the wood,
The moon wades deep in snow.
Pile balsam boughs about the sills,
And let the fires glow!

The cows must stand in the dark barn,
The horses stamp all day.
Now shall the housewife bake her pies
And keep her kitchen gay.

The cat sleeps warm beneath the stove,
The dog on paws outspread;
But the brown deer with flinching hide
Seeks for a sheltered bed.

The fox steps hungry through the brush,
The lean hawk coasts the sky.
"Winter is in the wood!" the winds
In the warm chimney cry.

12. *The Peddler*

"IS HE DEAD?" thought Sally, sitting in a corner of the room with her arms round Hannibal's neck for comfort. The uncles had carried the man in and laid him motionless on a bed. Between their bodies, leaning over him, Sally caught glimpses of a little man with a stubby beard and a face like a friendly monkey's, that had somehow been turned to marble.

"He *is* dead!" said Sally out loud, and began to cry softly.

"Hush!" whispered Aunt Deborah, hurrying by with some blankets. "He's not dead, child."

Sally caught at her skirt. "Will he be all right?" she whispered back.

"I don't know." Aunt Deborah spoke low as though the man might overhear her. "Let me go, dear. There's no time to be lost."

Outside all was still, but inside people were hurrying softly and speaking low quick directions. Sally, watching with her heart in her mouth, saw Uncle Eben force the man's mouth open with the top of the rum bottle, and a moment later she was brought to her feet by seeing the stranger's eyes open, in a bright blue stare that made her catch her breath. But she had little time to be relieved for Uncle Joseph just then came in with a pail full of snow. She saw him cutting off the man's shoes with his knife, and now they were all filling their hands with snow and the uncles were rubbing his feet with it and the aunts were rubbing his hands and nose and ears, while the man groaned and stirred.

"Poor man, isn't he cold enough?" thought Sally. "But Uncle Joseph and Aunt Nannie must know."

Hannibal, feeling the trouble all about him, began to whine.

"Oh, stop it, Hannibal," said Sally. "You *must* stop it."

The snow was getting low in the pail, and Sally took another one outdoors to fill. The hired men were walking the horses and oxen and cows up and down slowly while the struggle went on inside.

"How is the poor critter, Miss Sally?" asked Jehoshaphat Mountain, sympathetically.

"He's alive," said Sally. "But it's awful, Jehoshaphat Mountain—everyone's rubbing him with snow."

"So he won't lose his fingers and toes, that is," said Jehoshaphat. "They mustn't warm too quick or they would fall right off. A peddler, I think he is, from the pack we found beside him."

Sally hurried back with the snow. And now even she could see that the circulation was coming back into the man's veins, and his flesh no longer looked so like stone. But he was groaning worse than ever.

"Is he dying, Uncle Eben?" she asked, putting the pail handy.

"Not a bit of it, child," said Uncle Eben. "The blood's coming back, that's all. He'll be all right in two shakes of a lamb's tail. But get more snow, there's a good child. We want to save all of him, if we can."

Sally was out in the snow and back again like a flash. The peddler wasn't groaning so much now and everyone looked more cheerful.

"There, Esther," said Aunt Deborah, "his face is safe, I think. You'd better warm some more blankets now. How are his feet, Brother Joseph?"

"A few minutes more on this left one and his feet will be out of all danger too," Uncle Joseph replied.

The man spoke for the first time, whisperingly. "I'm sure I'm much obleeged to you all," he said. "Is my pack safe?"

"Safe as can be," answered Aunt Nannie with a kind smile.

"It's my living, ma'am," said the man, and fell soundly to sleep with his mouth open.

Uncle Joseph shook himself. "Well, now," said he, "since the peddler's attended to, poor man, we'd best be getting the cattle on, Eben." And the uncles bundled again into their heavy fur coats and clambered out, and soon the journey was resumed. Meantime, the aunts returned to their knitting, after Aunt Deborah had put some broth on the stove to heat.

"Like as not he'll want something hot when he wakes up," she said. There was an air of relief and satisfaction in the room that one could feel as truly as the heat of the fire.

Sally sat on the little stool, basking in it, with Hannibal blinking drowsily in the warmth. After a long while Dinah appeared from nowhere and climbed into her lap.

"Bad weather for peddling," said Aunt Nannie out of the peaceful silence.

"I suppose, Sister," said Aunt Deborah, "beggars can't be choosers. If he has no place of his own, he must earn his bread winter as well as summer."

"Poor man," said Aunt Esther, "I'm glad we found him in time. Half an hour more and we couldn't have done very much."

"It was Hannibal who found him, wasn't it, Hannibal?" said Sally from her stool.

"You're right, child, we mustn't forget Hannibal," said Aunt Esther, leaning over to rub the cub's head for a moment.

"You think he's good for something *now*, don't you, Aunt Nannie?" went on Sally.

Aunt Nannie looked up.

"Let this teach us all that we can never judge another," she said, solemnly. "Without Hannibal, the poor man would have died in his sleep, still sitting on that stone by the road. All the same," she added with a change of voice, "he smells dreadfully furry with the snow melting off him, my dear."

Late in the afternoon Sally looked up and found the peddler's bright blue eyes upon her. He was looking at

"Here you be, miss," he said, "at your service.
As fine a doll as ever I carried."

them all, wonderingly—at Sally and the cub, at the aunts knitting, at the painting on the wall.

"Now, I call this snug," he said in a voice that sounded surprisingly big and deep for such a small man. "Whar am I? The last I knowed, I was all beat out and almost froze a-trying to git to Nobleboro. Now here I be in bed and yit a-moving-like."

"Drink this broth," said Aunt Deborah, filling a bowl for him, "and Sally, dear, bring the gentleman a piece of bread and butter."

It was Aunt Nannie who told him who they were and how they had found him.

"So it was that thar angel child and her cub-b'ar lighted on me!" he exclaimed, and before anyone could stop him he had swung off the bed, draped in a couple of blankets, and limped over to the corner where his pack lay. He rummaged there for a moment, and drew out a large wooden doll with carnation-pink cheeks and black painted hair, dressed in the latest fashion.

"Here you be, miss," he said, "at your sarvice. As fine a doll as ever I carried, and proud to give her to my presarver. And here's a peppermint stick for the cub-b'ar, and to the ladies, my humble thanks. Mr. Burin is your sarvint, Miss and Miss and Miss," he went on, bowing with absurd dignity in his blankets.

Sally sat with the doll in her arms, for Dinah had jumped down from her lap at the approach of a stranger and slid like a shadow behind the stove. But Sally had no eye for Dinah, or for Hannibal, holding his peppermint stick between his paws and licking it delightedly. After a breathless thank-you to the peddler, she had given a quick look at Aunt Nannie, but Aunt Nannie was smiling. She might keep this wonderful doll, then! She had never had a doll like this before, only home-made ones that were little more than a billet of wood wrapped in a piece of cloth. But this doll was jointed at the shoulders and body and knees. She had painted hands and real leather shoes and petticoats like a person, and eyebrows arching over the blackest of eyes. Her expression was a little severe, but it did not seem so to Sally.

"Do you think Eunice would be a nice name?" she asked, out of a dream.

"A very nice name," said Aunt Esther.

Meantime, Mr. Burin had gone into the little room at the back to put on some of Uncle Eben's clothes which Aunt Nannie had lent to him, since his own were not dry yet. He came out spry as a cricket, and limped briskly to his pack.

"I'm so lame," he exclaimed cheerfully. "Tree fell on me when I was a boy. Killed my brother, it did. Here's books, pins, needles, black sewing-silk, all colors tape, varses, almanacs, an' sarmons, thread, fine thread for cambric ruffles, here's varses on the pirate that was hung on Boston Common, with a border of coffins atop, and 'Jack the Piper,' 'Whittington's Cat,' 'Pilgrim's Progress,' 'The History of the Devil,' an' a great many other religious books," he went on all in one breath.

The aunts hurried to light a candle—for darkness still came early on gray days—and were soon handling tapes and spools. Sally found the story of Whittington's cat and showed Eunice the pictures. They were all so busy that they did not notice when the house stopped, and looked up in surprise at the uncles' entrance. Mr. Burin had been doing a brisk trade.

"Glad to see you so well, sir," said Uncle Joseph in his friendly way. "We've arrived at Nobleboro and made our arrangements for the night. But I declare, no one in here has even noticed we've stopped, you're so taken up with pretties. Why, what's that you've got, Sally?" he asked, seeing Eunice for the first time. "A regular belle, she is. Will you introduce us, my dear?"

Uncle Eben's eyes danced with mischief. "It's Saturday evening after sundown, and the Sabbath has begun, Nannie," he said, delighted at a chance to tease his sister.

Aunt Nannie looked startled, but recovered quickly. "With all these clouds you can't tell for sure if the sun is down or not," she said firmly. "But I declare, we'd best do no more. We're late with our supper as it is. Bring in the milk as soon as you can, Brother, so we can get the chores done and the Sabbath properly begun."

Everyone hurried to finish supper, for it was the custom to have all work out of the way by sundown Saturday night. But the storm and the rescue had delayed everything. It was after seven when the last dish was clean and back in place. Now it was time for farewell.

"That's whar I was a-going, and that's whar I'm now a-getting, thanks to that thar angel child and her cub-b'ar," he said, a gentle look on his wrinkled face. "Whara'r you be, Miss, you know someone is wishing you well. And may that thar Eunice doll remind you sometimes of old Burin, the peddler. Your sarvint, everyone. I have to thank you if I'm alive this night!" And with this the peddler, with tears in his blue eyes, went off to sleep in the house near by, where he was well known.

When he was gone, Uncle Joseph sat wearily down with the big Bible open on his knees.

"May I hold Eunice if I don't play with her, please, Aunt Nannie, just this once?" asked Sally.

Aunt Nannie nodded. "Just this once, mind, child," she said.

All too soon it was eight o'clock, Saturday night bedtime. Uncle Joseph came out of his doze, to make a simple prayer, thanking God for having preserved them through the dangers of that day, and for having permitted them, by the aid of a wild beast of the forest, to save a human life. They all said "Amen" with all their hearts, and Uncle Joseph put on his coat and lit the lantern to take a last look at the tired cattle and the horses. Sally put on her cloak, too, and went with him, wrapping Eunice carefully in a fold of the cloth. Outdoors they stopped, struck by the cold stillness of the night. The trees were black on the silver of the snow, and the barn looked like a cave under its white roof. Over the house where the peddler slept hung the Pleiades, and a tree's bare branches were dark against a dew of stars.

Then a cow lowed and they stepped down into the cold velvet of the snow.

No leaf is left
To rustle faintly.
No stream is left
To sing and flow.
In silence night
Darkens the woodlands,
In silence the stars
Shine over the snow.
The cock that crowed
For dawn is voiceless,
The drowsy cattle
Stir and breathe deep,
And men that labored
Through all the daylight
With idle hands
Now fall asleep.

13. *Home*

THEY HAD crossed over the last of the rivers and just in time, for spring was surely coming now, and soon the ice would be breaking up and going out to the sea. There were patches of bare earth on some of the hills, and the snow in the road was discolored with mud.

"It will last our turn," said Uncle Joseph. "Keep the oxen at it, Jehoshaphat Mountain. They will have rest enough soon."

Sally knew that if all went well they would reach Pleasant Valley that day, and see the great Penobscot.

"There will be no more journeying, Eunice," she told the doll. "We will settle down and you shall play with my cousin Sophronia's doll, and Dinah can tell all her adventures to the cats of Maine. You've traveled, haven't you, Dinah, just like Dick Whittington's cat?"

Dinah, hearing her name, came and purred against

Sally's ankles, ignoring Eunice, of whom she was perhaps jealous. Hannibal was riding in the sleigh. A dozen times during the day Sally was out of the door of the little house and running forward to Uncle Joseph to ride pillion with him on Peacock, or running back to drive in the sleigh with Uncle Eben and Hannibal behind Dorcas. She couldn't keep still. She happened to be with Uncle Eben when a man on a roan horse with saddle-bags behind him overtook them and drew rein beside them.

He proved to be the doctor from Pleasant Valley, and after a few minutes' talk he raised his hat and rode on. It must have been he who spread the news of their arrival, for an hour or two later Sally, who at the time was fidgeting on a chair in the little house, heard a horse ride up at a gallop. Before one could say Jack Robinson, the door had been flung open, and there stood Cousin Sam Hallet with eyes only for Aunt Esther, who had jumped up from her chair and stood staring at him with her hand over her heart.

In two steps Cousin Sam had crossed the room and taken her in his arms, where she seemed quite willing to be.

"Why, I declare!" said Aunt Nannie, laughing, while her ear-drops jingled. "You'd better say how-do-you-do to the rest of us, Sam, before you both forget we're alive."

Sally turned to Eunice. "There'll be a wedding before the trees at Tuggie Noyes' have turned yellow again," she said, "and I'll make you a white dress and there'll be a cake and everything."

Then the others rode up—Cousin Ephraim, red-faced and hearty, and young John, and Sophronia, her fair hair curling from under a coonskin cap.

By this time, the oxen had stopped and the men stood grinning as they leaned against their poles. And of course both the uncles had hurried into the little house.

"You look like one of the patriarchs in the midst of his herds, Joseph!" Cousin Ephraim exclaimed, shaking him by the hand. John went about examining the room.

"My dearest Sally," cried Sophronia, embracing her, "I have been counting the days for you. I'm stitching you a sampler, too, with a motto I made up, myself:

We now see Sally Smith again,
The thing we've waited for.
May we live happy in dear Maine
Full fifty years or more!

I think that's the way it goes. La! what a lucky girl you are to travel in a traveling house all of your own! And there's your picture! I declare, you look like a princess. Did you see Sachem, my pony? He's a beauty and you'll love Antic and—"

Sophronia was so stored up with things to say that Sally would never have been able to answer if someone in the confusion hadn't stepped on the tip of Dinah's tail that was just sticking out from under the bed. Dinah went off like a bunch of fire-crackers, and it took a good deal of petting from Sally and Sophronia before she smoothed down her ruffled hair and Sally had a chance to show the beauties of Eunice and boast about their own cub who saved people's lives.

The riding horses had been tied behind the little house and Uncle Joseph gave the order to start. Sophronia was enraptured. "What will everyone say when they know I have been riding in a real cottage?" she said. "See how things go by the windows! It's the most beautiful game I ever played. John, was there ever anything like it?"

John grinned shyly and shook his head. He was a thin boy of about thirteen, as quiet as Sophronia was talkative, but he had eyes that saw everything and looked straight at people. He was enjoying himself quite as much as his sister, and Sally, seeing everything afresh through their eyes, was as much excited as on the day when she had first seen the little house come out of the woods.

"Suppose, Sophronia, you help Sally prepare tea," suggested Aunt Nannie. "This is our first party, Cousin Ephraim."

Sophronia laid out the dishes while Sally prepared the six little pots with coffee, with chocolate, with old Hyson, with new Hyson, with Souchong, and with chocolate and milk. Sophronia was enraptured at the sight but, seeing her father's eye on her, said nothing. Cousin Ephraim was looking more out of the window, however, than at his daughter.

All of a sudden he cried out in a clear voice: "Joseph, have the oxen stop! Put on your cloaks, all of you, and tumble out. I have something to show you."

In a moment the little house was empty. Even Dinah had slipped out and sat on the doorstep, blinking. It was late afternoon and the sky was primrose colored over their heads. They stood, the little house and its oxen, the huddled cows, the horses and sleds and Hannibal in the sleigh, the hired men, and the group of grown-ups and children, holding their cloaks about them, on top of a hill. The country sloped gently away from them in long billows of natural pasture and woodland to a broad river far below. The pools along the surface of the ice reflected back the primrose of the sky, but gleaming and fluid. Far away, the hills on the horizon rose in blue bubbles against the sky, and there was a village at the edge of the water, with a church steeple and smoke rising straight and pale from the chimneys of the houses.

A hush fell on everyone. The beauty of the scene in that light was unreal and breathless. Everyone drank it in, absorbed. No one spoke.

It was Cousin Ephraim who at last broke the silence, but even he spoke in a subdued voice.

"That's Pleasant Valley," he said, making a gesture towards the village below them, "and this—"

He paused and they all waited.

"And this," he went on, "this is yours if you want it, Joseph."

"This?" asked Aunt Nannie with a sort of sigh. "Can a person own this?"

"A thousand acres, down to the river and as far east as we can see," said Cousin Ephraim.

Sally took Uncle Joseph's hand. It was trembling.

"I say with Nannie," he murmured at last, "can a person own this?"

So they stood a little longer until the light faded and it was time to go down where Cousin Jennie waited dinner for them in the town.

"Let's go with the horses," suggested Aunt Nannie. "Then the house will seem like home waiting for us when we come back."

And so it was that Sally in the sleigh, with Eunice under one arm and Dinah under the other, looking back, saw dark against the stars the little house on runners, its travels over, standing at last securely upon their own land.

The past was good, but ahead there lie
Blue hills and rivers reflecting the sky
And soil that has never known the plow
Down all the millions of years, until now.
The oxen walk with a quiet tread—
Was that some stone, or an arrowhead
They disturbed in passing? Soon fields of corn
Will stand here, barbaric in the morn,
And the wind will go running down the wheat,
And men and beasts shall have food to eat;
And a child who is wandering all alone
May find mushrooms as round as a wave-worn stone,
Or gather strawberries small and red,
Or glimpse a deer with its antlered head,
Or leaning against the pasture bars,
May stare towards the west at the early stars.
All, all awaits. Up hill, down valley—
The time is ripe, and away goes Sally!

About the Author

Elizabeth Coatsworth has been a well-known name in children's literature for many decades. She was born in 1893 and her first book was published in 1927 just as separate departments for children's books were being established in American publishing. Her last book for children was published in 1975, eleven years before her death in 1986. In 1931 she won the Newbery Medal for *The Cat Who Went to Heaven,* a book inspired by her many travels and her "painter's eye for color and form" that had been so evident in her earlier books of poetry for adults. Her fellow Vassar classmate and the first children's book editor at Macmillan's, Louise Seaman Bechtel, wrote, "She took on her journeys a brilliant mind, a flair for the strange and picturesque, a lively interest in all kinds of people. She gradually discovered, in the years that followed, many ways to interpret her emotional and intellectual response to far places, in prose and verse." *(Newbery Medal Books: 1922-1955).* Though this Newbery Award title has remained in print, the author became known and loved by many readers more through her succeeding work—including the stories and often-cited poetry in the five volumes about Sally.

Despite the fact that Elizabeth Coatsworth was born in Buffalo, New York, and began a lifetime of world traveling at the age of five, she gave her heart to New England, particularly the state of Maine. It is here that many of her more than 90 books are centered. Her husband, writer and naturalist Henry Beston whom she married in 1929, and her two daughters, Margaret and Catherine, shared her love for their farm in Maine.

The five acclaimed "Sally" books are a happy blend of a keen historical and geographical feel for both New England and its place in the larger world in the years after the American Revolution. In the author's own words she tried to "give some of the exciting aspects of a life at once civilized and lived on a frontier near the sea, when our trade was just expanding." Ruth Hill Viguers further writes about the "Sally" books in *A Critical History of Children's History:*

> Elizabeth Coatsworth also recaptured for children the enchantment she has long felt for Maine. . . Her first period story, *Away Goes Sally* (1934), made the most of the entrancing idea of living in a little house on runners, slowly sliding through the snowy New England roads and forests, drawn by twelve strong oxen, to transport its occupants from Massachusetts to a new home in Maine. A great deal of kindly humor is woven throughout the story of Sally and her aunts and uncles and with the many lively events are glimpses of the quiet beauty of the New England winter. Some of Miss Coatsworth's loveliest poetry is to be found between the chapters of this and other books, but her prose, too, is that of a poet, lucent and concise. Four other books about Sally followed as her heroine grew up: *Five Bushel Farm* (1939), *The Fair American* (1940), *The White Horse* (1942), and *The Won-*

> *derful Day* (1946). There is no sacrifice of reality in the more colorful plots and settings of these stories. The clarity of style carries conviction, and, with no extra words the reader is kept aware of the excitement in beauty everywhere, the friendly comfort of life on the well-loved Maine farm, the joy of being aboard a trim ship with salt wind on one's face, the strange magic of North Africa and alien ways.

Another source has this to say about the appealing interpersonal landscape which is also an authentic aspect of the geographical and social period:

> *Away Goes Sally* (1934) introduces us to an early 19th century family of three sisters and two brothers who are raising an orphaned niece. The interplay of family relationships is excellent . . . All the small details of living are interestingly worked into the stories; the children are obedient but resourceful; family cooperation is the normal state of affairs.
>
> *(Children and Books, Fifth edition)*

This portrayal of family loyalty and love, not the less strong for often being undemonstrative, is of particular worth today in laying down an imaginative foundation for hope and encouragement in a world where such things are no longer clearly delineated.

It should come as no surprise that the works of Elizabeth Coatsworth, with their intelligent simplicity and picture-evoking poetry of language, continue to demonstrate a timeless appeal to the host of new readers, both young and old, of today.

More Stories About Sally

Five Bushel Farm

Aunt Esther marries, Aunt Debbie finds a "son," Uncle Eben is as jolly and as lazy as ever, Uncle Joseph is busy felling trees for the new house and Aunt Nannie contrives to make a home for all in the wilderness. When Andrew joins the household, Sally finally has someone her own age to work and play with. It is they who find the perfect spot for the new house and they who make the friends, which, in the end, ensure its safety.

The Fair American

While Five Bushel Farm is prospering on one side of the Atlantic Ocean, there is turmoil and destruction on the other side. When Sally, with Andrew and her Aunt Debbie, sail to France on the *Fair American*, she is unexpectedly drawn into the sorrows and the bittersweet joys of a people and land at war with itself.

The White Horse

After one adventurous, but fairly safe voyage, Aunt Nannie reluctantly allows Sally to sail away again, this time into the Mediterranean Sea—and right into the clutches of the Barbary Coast pirates. Taken captive, Sally is exposed to a way of life very different from the protected one she has known. Her resiliency as well as her courage and love are sorely tried; however, both she and those she encounters in the Sultan's palace will never be quite the same for her stay there.

The Wonderful Day

It is four years after the *Fair American* has returned from France and now Pierre, whom they'd met on their adventures there, is to visit Five Bushel Farm for the first time. Sally is so happily caught up in the pleasure of his coming and in the preparations for the celebratory dance, she fails to notice Uncle Joseph's forced smiles or Andrew's increasing grimness. Though calamity is lurking behind the clouds of this most wonderful day, a longstanding friendship, a race against time, and a meeting of hearts bring the day to its satisfying close